ISBN: 9798843890629

Find other works by this author: https://twitter.com/RHardpole

1st Edition. Published August 2022

Fluid Bonded

RODNEY
HARDPOLE

For Ophelia

For turning fantasies into reality.

Hayden let out a long, satisfied groan. Jessica could feel her partners body shudder from head to toe as he pumped his thick load deep into her quivering slit. The muscular walls of her pussy spasmed as she milked his throbbing cock for every drop of his fertile seed. God, it felt good! No, it felt more than good. It felt fucking fantastic! It felt better than anything she had ever felt before in the whole world.

At nineteen, Jessica was not entirely inexperienced in the bedroom, but this was the first time she had felt a man ejaculate inside her. It had been nearly two years ago that she had lost her virginity to Ethan, her boyfriend from high school and, to date that had been her only long-term relationship. The couple had always been meticulous regarding the practice of safe sex and had never failed to wear condoms. Their relationship was not destined to last having eventually broken down the previous summer as they both got places at separate universities Ethan had accepted a place down in Glasgow whilst Jessica's chosen course was best suited across the country in Aberdeen.

Although initially heartbroken it had not taken Jessica too long to begin enjoying the sexual liberation that came with being a student living away from home and it was not as if she found herself facing a shortage of suitors. Jessica was a bonnie lass, as a child her mother used to pinch her cheek then tap her on the nose and call her "cute as a button!" She hailed from the highlands of Scotland and had grown up in and around Fort William, a small but significant town on the West Coast in the shadow of Ben Nevis.

Jessica possessed the genetics of a stereotypical Scot. She was a fiery redhead with jade green eyes and of a fair complexion. Her skin was peppered with freckles, which would redden and burn with even the slightest exposure to the summer sun. She wore a size 12 (based on her favourite pair of skinny stretchy H&M Jeans!) Mostly she found herself more comfortable in a 14, but she carried her weight well, at 5ft 9 and with voluptuous breasts and a rounded, peachy behind she possessed a beautifully curvy figure that never failed to turn heads.

The night she met Hayden had been no exception. Jessica and her friends had spent the evening at Vesuvius, a large live music venue with an accompanying trendy cocktail bar called Sleaze! down on the quayside. They had initially gone to see SKArred and Bruised, a touring band whose name aptly described their style and that had a reputation for setting a lively party atmosphere. The band did not disappoint, and by the time they had finished their set, Jessica and her friends were in no mood to go home. Instead, the party had moved on to the adjacent Sleaze! bar where the drinking and dancing continued into the wee hours.

It was here that Hayden had caught her eye. He was not a total stranger; Aberdeen was a reasonably small city. Not small enough that everyone knew everyone, but small enough that the faces that showed up every student night. Were familiar. Hayden was on the periphery of their extended group out that evening, Although Jessica had never spoken to him before she knew him as a friend of a friend of a friend.

Hayden was of a fairly shy nature, he had always been the quiet, studious type, but he had been persuaded to come out that evening to watch the band and was still hanging about, mainly to share in the cost of a taxi back with his flatmates. After a number of beers though, he had finally plucked up the Dutch courage to approach Jessica and offered to buy her drink.

Jessica clearly pleased with the attention, readily accepted and offered to accompany him to the bar to help, partially out of politeness, but also, a chance to get some alone time with this handsome man. Besides, Jessica was always cautious on a night out never to let a drink out of her sight. The student union had run a campaign warning that in the past there had been a spate of students who had their drinks spiked sand Jessica was not the type of girl to take unnecessary risk.

Hayden, she soon discovered was a fellow student, also in his second year studying Geology and Petroleum engineering living in digs just a little further out of town than her own. He was tall, but slim with stylish dark hair. He was freshly shaven and had the sort of boyish good looks that the quiet, brooding member of a boyband might possess.

As they waited to get served Jessica utilised all her flirtatious tricks to indicate her interest, running her fingers through her ginger locks, maintaining eye contact, laughing at his attempt at a humour. She gave him her undivided attention.

Hayden handed her the drink and Jessica raised her glass in a toast, "Slàinte mhath!" They both took a swig from their cocktails. Student nights were always 2 for 1 on cocktails even when they had bands on. Jessica let the flavour linger on her palette, slowly licking her lips. Hayden got the message and when it finally came to kicking out time Jessica offered him a spare seat in her cab. Hayden no longer held any intention of going to his own home that night!

Jessica lay on the bed. Her post orgasmic bliss was beginning to subside. Hayden was still on top of her, still inside her. His spent cock beginning to shrink as his blood flow redirected. He had collapsed onto her, exhausted. His limp weight pressed down on her and was starting to feel uncomfortable. The reality of her situation now began to set in and it began to dawn on her that she had not actually allowed him to cum inside her. In fact, she had expressly forbidden it.

"What the hell have you done?" Jessica questioned her lover whilst pushing him aside. Hayden's softening cock slipped out of her pussy leaving a sticky wet trail cross her thigh and a damp sticky patch in the fiery red thatch of her neatly trimmed pubic hair as he rolled off her to lay beside her.

"You promised to pull out?" she continued; her voice was becoming stern as the feeling of bliss subsided and quickly turned to anger.

"Er… I guess I was just enjoying it so much that in the height of it all I forgot!" Hayden was most probably lying. Jessica reasoned that. he clearly had no intention of pulling out. It was the oldest trick in the book and she had fallen for it hook, line and sinker.

"You don't need to worry, I'm clean." Hayden added. The University of Aberdeen held the undesirable accolade of having the highest rate of sexually transmitted infections not just in Scotland but in the entire United Kingdom. A statistic that perhaps comes as no surprise considering the cities status as the main port servicing the workers of the North Sea Oil fields. Out on the rigs for weeks if not months at a time, as soon as they hit the shore it was straight into the pubs, clubs and brothels that surrounded the dockside. Aberdeen had always had a seedy reputation for vice. Regardless, Hayden's response was unlikely to offer much in the way of reassurance. "You are on the pill, aren't you?" He finally enquired.

This question infuriated Jessica. *Why hadn't the horny bastard thought to ask that before he fucked me!* Jessica had asked him on more than one occasion to wear a condom but he had come up with the usual rubbish excuses about having an allergic reaction to the latex and not being able to feel it properly. Jessica knew it was bullshit, she should have said no but in the end had allowed herself to be persuaded. Anyway, he had promised to withdraw before he came. She felt stupid for believing him.

"No, I'm not on the fucking pill!" Jessica snapped. "That's why I wanted you to wear the bloody Johnny!"

"Well, I suppose you can go get the morning after pill?" Hayden suggested. This only angered Jessica further, her blood began to boil. She had taken emergency contraception once before when a condom had torn and it had given her not only terrible stomach cramps over the following days but throughout her next period as well.

"I suppose I'm going to have to." Jessica spat out "It's just I get really bad side effects from the hormones in them, but I suppose it's better than having to put up with a latex allergy!" she added sarcastically.

"Look if there's anything I can do?" Hayden offered partly out of guilt, partly out of courtesy but mainly because he knew there was little he could do.

He was soon to discover how wrong he was.

J essica hadn't planned what she was about to say. She had no idea that her next few words would mark the start of a new chapter in both of their lives. She certainly didn't mean anything by them she was just angry when she allowed the following words to slip out.

"You want to help?" Jessica spat the words out laced with vitriol. She was angry at Hayden for lying. She was angry at him for being a man and having it so much easier when it came to sex, but mainly she was angry at herself for being so gullible. "What exactly are you going to do?" The question was of course, rhetorical. Surely the tone in which she delivered them indicated as much. But she continued, "Suck yer cum out ma gash?"

A short but awkward silence followed as Hayden comprehended Jessica's apparent request.

"Okay then." he mumbled quietly and meekly. Then slowly, but without further hesitation he reluctantly went down on her.

This was not the response that Jessica had expected. Not that she had expected a response but nevertheless she allowed her legs to part as Hayden's head moved towards her sex. *Just get on with it!* Hayden told himself. There was no point dragging this out. He had gotten his end away without considering the consequences and now he was just going to have to deal with his mess.

As Jessica opened her legs the strong scent of their stale sex hit him with an immediacy that quickly brought him to his senses but it was too late to back away now. He extended his tongue and began to tentatively lick at her vulva.

Hayden soon discovered the taste was not as repulsive as he had feared and gaining in confidence, he began to trace the sides of her opening, cleaning out the fleshy folds of her labia before moving his tongue around her clit. Jessica let out a contented sigh and relaxed her body. *Oh boy! This guy really knows how to use his tongue!* Hayden continued to circle her clit with the tip of his tongue, soon Jessica began to anticipate his rhythm and began to buck her hips to meet him.

Hayden could feel Jessica's pulse throbbing through her engorged clit, accompanied by the sound of her appreciative moans encouraged him to explore further. He thrust his tongue deep inside her delving and probing as he circled her inner depth. He scooped up a mouthful of what was surely his own cum. The taste was not as strong as he had expected, slightly salty with a metallic tang, but it was not that which concerned him. It was the texture that he disliked. His mouth was filled with a slimy, viscous and gloopy sludge that he was unable to swallow. He tried to shift it around his mouth away from his taste buds, pushing it away with the tip of his tongue and storing it in the side of his cheek. It was all he could do to keep from gagging. He tried to move his head away from Jessica's pussy and turn to one side in an attempt to discreetly dispose of the offending substance by spitting it out on the sheets.

Jessica was enjoying herself way too much to pause, she could feel an orgasm building and at the very moment Hayden tried to pull his head away, Jessica grabbed him by his hair and with both hands pulled his face up tight against her pussy.

"Oh aye, keep your tongue right there!" Jessica Exclaimed!

Hayden attempted to protest but, in his position the only sound he was able to produce was a muffled sigh. He was now left with no choice but to clear his throat and swallow his own load. Jessica felt him gulp it down and encouraged him to continue.

"Oh yes, suck all your cum out of my dirty pussy!" she demanded "Clean me up! Every last drop! I don't want to fall pregnant!"

All this dirty talk was turning Hayden on. Despite it only having been a few minutes since his own orgasm, his cock had already stiffened. He responded by plunging his tongue as deep into her pussy as he could. There was no doubting nor denying it, he was definitely relishing this task. Jessica sensed his newly found enthusiasm and responded by contracting her pelvic floor muscles, squeezing out another wad of cum that had been lodged deep inside her womb. Smaller than the last and less viscous, mixed as it was with her own juices which were now flowing freely. Hayden eagerly lapped up the combination of their sweet secretions before returning to suck at her wet hole.

All this was too much for Jessica. It was driving her over the edge.

"Please don't stop, I'm going to cum!" Jessica begged, bucking her hips and thrusting her pussy against her lover's face. Her orgasm came in like a stormy tide, pulsating waves, rising and falling, each one larger than the last. She reached her peak and at the crest of the largest wave she finally lost control. Her body tensed as she squirted her own juices forcefully over Hayden's face.

Hayden opened his mouth wide to catch all he could of her precious nectar. Flowing past his taste buds he found her scent was inoffensive and the taste was mild. Jessica came so hard it was impossible to distinguish if she was still squirting or actually urinating. Hayden no longer cared. He soon found his mouth was full and so he closed it, swallowing hurriedly so as to waste as little as possible. He quickly opened his mouth again with a gasp. Still her juice was flowing. There was no doubt remaining she was pissing directly into his mouth! Hayden could not care less he eagerly drank from her as she washed all remnants of his fertile seed from her womb.

At last, her stream began to subside fading into intermittent spurts that Hayden gratefully lapped up. Jessica caught her breath and her senses. She looked down at the mess of the man between her legs and began to assess the situation she had found herself in. His face and hair were soddened, soaked in her own piss. She had totally lost control. She could feel the heat in her face as the blood flowed to the surface, she knew her pale skin was reddening betraying her embarrassment of this situation in which she now found herself.

What now? Should she apologise for her accident? Make him promise to never say another word on the matter? Throw him out and hope she would never bump into him again?

No. Jessica noticed that Hayden's cock was still rock hard in his hand. He was beating away it furiously. He had drunk from her willingly. He had clearly enjoyed every minute.

Never in a million years had she imagined that this clean-cut boy would be so eager to please that he would do what he had just done. He had worked his magic with his tongue. He didn't just clean out her pussy, he had worshipped it. No, she would be a fool not to take advantage of such a man.

"You seemed to like that?" Jessica enquired.

Hayden looked up suddenly conscious that he was still masturbating. There was no point denying it. He had. "I've never done anything like that before." Hayden replied truthfully. "But it was so kinky!"

"Well, yer can empty ya bawbags in me anytime" Jessica offered with a smirk and a glint in her eye. "As long as ya promise to clean me oot again!"

Hayden did not need telling twice. He was more than ready to go again and satisfied with her consent he slid up between her legs and with no more than a slight guide of the hand thrust his stiff cock deep into her wet, willing pussy. Jessica gasped as he filled her once more, reaching right up against her cervix with his first thrust. She could smell her own sex all over him and it was driving her wild with lust. She reached her arms around him and pulled him into her. Running her hand across the back of his head and down his back, his hair was damp with their shared fluids. He began to pound away with an animalistic eagerness he had not shown earlier.

Jessica began to pant and moan in response, each thrust seemed harder and to reach deeper than the last.

"Owh yes, fuck me raw!" Jessica cried. "I want to feel ya pump your seed into me!"

Hayden responded to this encouragement by driving her deep into her mattress.

"I can'nee get pregnant though!" Jessica warned "You'll have to clean me oot!"

The thought of this was pushing Hayden over the edge once more. This time though he knew what was expected of him. As soon as he came, he would have to lick her clean again. This time however, he desired it, he craved it, he wanted nothing else but to devour it. He couldn't wait to taste her again, to taste himself, to share their own homemade cocktail. To savour its complex flavours.

He would have to do an exceptional job. If even the tiniest microscopic sperm cell remained, if just one dedicated swimmer persevered, he ran the risk of impregnating her.

Hayden was barely twenty. They were both at the peak of their fertility and Hayden was certainly not ready to become a father especially with a girl he had only just met a few hours previously. The fear only exited him further. He was about to blow once more planting his seed deep inside her, where it would all too easily propagate. Jessica could sense it and she wanted it.

She dug her nails into his back whilst arching her own, turning her head to bite the pillow as she was driven again to her own orgasm. Her body tensed and shuddered.

"Cum for me now!" Jessica commanded.

Hayden obliged. Shooting a fresh load of his baby batter deep inside her. He slid out pulling a pail marbled trail of cum with him. Hayden sat upright to take in the scene. The delicious looking creampie dripping from out of her swollen pussy. Hayden licked his lips at the tasty delicacy that lay before him.

"Eat me!" Jessica demanded. Pushing his head downwards towards his prize.

Hayden once again obliged.

It was gone eleven the following morning when Hayden finally left Jessica's apartment to complete his walk of shame. He exchanged a polite but shy greeting as he acknowledged Jessica's flatmate, Sadia in the hall She responded by looking him up and down before giving him a knowing smile. He was not the first stranger to let himself out the morning after the night before. There was no point in even pretending to sneak him out. Jessica had practically screamed the house down the night before so Sadia was well aware she had scored. In fact it wouldn't surprise her if the neighbours had heard them too!

Before Hayden left, they had both made sure to exchange their contact details. Surely this had to be more than just a one-night stand? Now that they were fluid bonded. Could she trust him? Jessica was not sure about that. He had lied to her about pulling out. Jessica had already decided that this guy was probably not boyfriend material. One night stands never are, but nevertheless here she had a man that she would be a fool to let go of. If she played her cards right, she knew he would do whatever she desired.

She was going to have some fun with this one.

Other Erotic short stories available by Rodney Hardpole

A Day in The Life of a Toilet Slave

Another Day in The Life of a Toilet Slave

Pandora's Box

A Desperate Journey

Under Kates Command

Further Under Kates Command

Deeper Under Kates Command

Completely Under Kates Command

Sit On My Face and Clean Me Up!

Printed in Great Britain
by Amazon